3800 18 0054793 1
HIGH LIFE HIGHLAND

Tiny Aliens

KT-146-978

and the
Great Big Pet Disaster

Debbie White

ILLUSTRATED BY
Aleksei Bitskoff

HIGH LIFE HIGHLAND LIBRARIES	
38001800547931	
BERTRAMS	22/02/2019
	£4.99
JF	

WITHDRAWN

OXFORD
UNIVERSITY PRESS

OXFORD
UNIVERSITY PRESS

Great Clarendon Street, Oxford, OX2 6DP,
United Kingdom

Oxford University Press is a department of the University of Oxford.
It furthers the University's objective of excellence in research, scholarship,
and education by publishing worldwide. Oxford is a registered trade mark of
Oxford University Press in the UK and in certain other countries

Text © Debbie White 2017
Illustrations © Aleksei Bitskoff 2017

The moral rights of the author have been asserted

First published in this edition 2019

All rights reserved. No part of this publication may be reproduced, stored
in a retrieval system, or transmitted, in any form or by any means, without
the prior permission in writing of Oxford University Press, or as expressly
permitted by law, by licence or under terms agreed with the appropriate
reprographics rights organization. Enquiries concerning reproduction outside
the scope of the above should be sent to the Rights Department, Oxford
University Press, at the address above.

You must not circulate this work in any other form
and you must impose this same condition on any acquirer

British Library Cataloguing in Publication Data
Data available

978-0-19-276913-8

1 3 5 7 9 10 8 6 4 2

Paper used in the production of this book is a natural, recyclable product
made from wood grown in sustainable forests. The manufacturing process
conforms to the environmental regulations of the country of origin.

Printed in China

Helping your child to read

Before they start

- Talk about the back cover blurb. What kind of trouble might two Teeny Tiny Aliens get into?

- Look at the front cover. Can your child think of three words to describe the aliens?

During reading

- Let your child read at their own pace, either silently or out loud.
- If necessary, help them to work out words they don't know by saying each sound out loud and then blending them to say the word, e.g. *m-ou-n-t-ai-n-s, mountains.*
- Encourage your child to keep checking that the text makes sense and they understand what they are reading. Remind them to re-read to check the meaning if they're not sure.
- Give them lots of praise for good reading!

After reading

- Look at page 64 for some fun activities.

Chapter One

This is the faraway planet, Zap. It looks a bit like Earth. Except the rivers and seas are orange and the mountains are pink.

It's home to the Teeny Tiny Aliens, who are just like us. Except they only have three fingers on each hand and three toes on each foot ... and they are purple. And instead of hair, they have lovely wavy tentacles (a bit like teeny tiny elephant trunks).

This is Chief Big Teeny Tiny. He's in charge. He wears a teeny tiny T-shirt, which says CHIEF on it in big letters.

These are the Chief's little cousins, Itsy Teeny Tiny and Weeny Teeny Tiny. The Chief thinks they should wear T-shirts that say TROUBLE.

Itsy and Weeny don't mean to upset the Chief. They want to *help* him but, somehow, things always go wrong. Like the time the Chief was poorly with the spiffle spots (itchy spots that glow in the dark and change colour).

"He needs cheering up," said Itsy. "Having spiffle spots is no fun at all."

"Let's look up spiffle spots on the computer and see what will help," said Weeny.

Monster Guide to Alien Spots

Got spiffle spots? Try Womple Juice!

WOMPLE JUICE

WARNING! Must not be mixed with Pongee Crystals

So that night, Itsy and Weeny filled the Chief's bubble tub with lots of nice, hot, orange water and an *enormous* glug of Womple Juice.

"You look tired," said Weeny to the Chief.

"Warm bubbly water with Womple Juice will make you feel *much* better," said Itsy. "And why not put in some of your favourite Pongee Crystals?"

"What a lovely idea," said the Chief, getting into his bubble tub and pressing the bubble button.

"Aaah, bliss," he said. "Well done, Itsy and Weeny. My spiffle spots have stopped itching."

Itsy and Weeny were very pleased.

"Now for those Pongee Crystals," said the Chief, sprinkling them on to the bubbly water.

The water got bubblier …

and bubblier …

and bubblier.

Oops!

The bubbles rose up and covered the Chief. They filled the bubble tub. Then the whole room was full of bubbles … and the bubbles were heading out of the door. So were Itsy and Weeny. They'd just remembered what the *Monster Guide to Alien Spots* had said about mixing Womple Juice with Pongee Crystals …

DON'T!

"Come back, you pesky teeny tinies!" shouted the Chief as he jumped out of the bubble tub … and slipped right over. Crash! Bang! Ouch!

Poor Chief Big Teeny Tiny. He'd banged his elbow, hurt his bottom and his tentacles were bruised black and blue. He was *very* cross.

"Just wait until I catch up with you, Itsy and Weeny!"

An hour later, Itsy and Weeny were standing in front of Chief Big Teeny Tiny.

"We're really, really sorry, aren't we, Weeny?" said Itsy.

"Really, really sorry," said Weeny.

"You're always sorry!" bellowed the Chief. "Then you do something silly again! This time, take your Teeny Tiny Submarine to the bottom of the Teeny Tiny Sea for a whole week," said the Chief. "And *next* time you do something silly, I'm going to banish you from Zap!"

Chapter Two

Itsy and Weeny didn't enjoy being at
the bottom of the Teeny Tiny Sea. It was
dark down there, and very boring.

Except on the *very last* day, when a
Great Green Slurp Bubbler sneaked up
and tried to swallow their Teeny Tiny
Submarine. Luckily, Itsy and Weeny
saw it just in time!

Phew! They'd escaped being slurped *and* they were back in time for Chief Big Teeny Tiny's birthday party.

"I've got this amazing idea for his birthday present. The Chief's been saying for ages that he wants a pet," said Weeny.

"Let's get him two!" said Itsy.

So Itsy and Weeny went off and bought a pair of lovely little bug-eyed ziplets (plus zip-basket).

Then they went to the Teeny Tiny Bakery and ordered the Chief a special birthday cake. It had a hole cut out of the middle (for the ziplets to hide in). It had a pop-off lid (so the ziplets could pop up out of the cake) *and* it was covered in green slime icing. Yummy!

"He'll be so excited when he sees the ziplets jump out of the cake," said Itsy.

"Easy peasy womple squeezy. One, two, three, ta-dah!" said Weeny.

"What on Zap can go wrong *this* time?" said Itsy.

The Chief's birthday party started well. DJ Teeny Tiny Smalls was playing the Chief's favourite teeny tiny music tracks.

There were games (hunt the tromble, pin the tail on the wobblebuck and tentacle braiding).

16

There were scrumptious things to eat. Then finally it was time for Itsy and Weeny to bring in the cake.

The Chief looked very pleased when he saw it. "Green slime icing, my favourite! Thank you," he said.

"But this is the best bit," said Weeny.

"One, two, three!" shouted Itsy, popping the lid off the cake.

Well, it is true that ziplets make
lovely pets … as long as they don't eat
green slime icing. All that sugar makes
them go *super* zippy.

Oops!

Zipzipzipzipzipzip!

The ziplets took
off like rockets.

Green slime icing was flying everywhere (and mostly landing on the Chief). Chief Big Teeny Tiny looked like something from the bottom of a big green slimy pond.

"Catch those ziplets, Itsy and Weeny, then come and see me!" shouted the Chief. My word, the Chief was very angry.

Poor Itsy and Weeny. They sat in the middle of the floor and watched the ziplets zipping everywhere. The ziplets were moving so fast they were just a blur.

"We'll never catch them," said Weeny. "They're much too zippy."

But luckily, after a bit, the ziplets ran out of zip. They fell fast asleep in a corner, snoring loudly. Phew! Itsy and Weeny quickly popped them in the zip-basket.

Then they went to say sorry to
Chief Big Teeny Tiny.

"We thought you'd be pleased
with your present," said Weeny.

"You said you wanted a pet!"
said Itsy.

"We didn't know what would
happen," said Itsy and Weeny together.

"You never do! I've had enough," said
the Chief. "You're banished. Take your
Teeny Tiny Spaceship and leave Zap at
once. And take those ziplets with you!
I want a proper pet, not two annoying
little fuzz balls!"

Chapter Three

Soon poor Weeny and Itsy (and the ziplets) were drifting out in space in their Teeny Tiny Spaceship.

"I'm so miserable. Look, my skin has lost its purple glow! I just want to go home," said Itsy.

Poor Itsy did look very unhappy.

"Don't worry, I've got an ace idea," said Weeny. "Why don't we find Chief Big Teeny Tiny a pet so amazing he'll forgive us and let us go home?"

"Good thinking," said Itsy, brightening up. "Let's look up the *Teeny Tiny Monster Guide to Pets of the Universe*."

Weeny thought the Five-Horned Plip Monster from the planet Plip looked awesome.

Weeny read the description. "Must have a good supply of its favourite food: Teeny Tiny Aliens."

Oops!

"Well, how about the Bat-Eared
Gargler from the planet Gargle?"
said Itsy.

"When asleep, the Bat-Eared Gargler
makes a loud gargling noise. This causes
its owners to go deaf!" Weeny read.

Oops! Chief Big Teeny Tiny wouldn't
be happy about that.

Then, just as Itsy and Weeny were
starting to feel glum, a pet from the
planet Earth popped up on screen.

Itsy and Weeny read the description
together. "This pet makes a wonderful
friend. It is very intelligent and gentle.
It can carry its owner long distances on
its back."

Hurray!

Itsy and Weeny tapped 'How do we get to Earth?' into the spaceship's Teeny Tiny Computer.

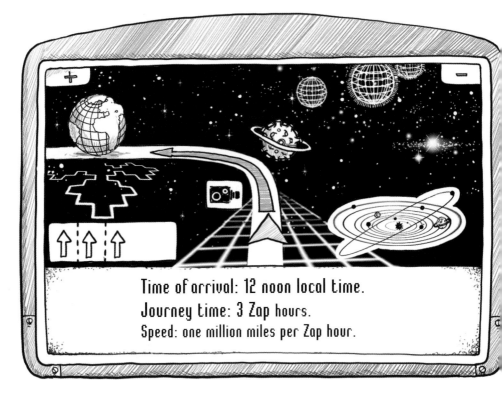

Time of arrival: 12 noon local time.
Journey time: 3 Zap hours.
Speed: one million miles per Zap hour.

Then they set off, not even stopping for breakfast.

At 12 noon, they landed safely on planet Earth.

Ping! The spaceship door opened and Itsy and Weeny (and the ziplets) popped out into a forest of green.

"Zapping Zoozies!" said Weeny. "It's going to be hard to spot our pet in here!"

"Don't worry," said Itsy, "I've got a picture of it. *And* we can use our Teeny Tiny Tracking Device."

So off they set.

They swished their
way through the
green forest.
They hid
from fearsome
monsters with
scary pincers and
lots of legs. At last the
Teeny Tiny Tracking Device
said: "You have reached your pet."

Itsy and Weeny walked around and
around in circles looking for it.

"Where is it?" said Weeny, giving the
tracking device a good hard thump.

Poor Teeny Tinies, they *were*
worn out.

"Let's take a teeny tiny nap," said Itsy, "and then carry on looking."

"Good idea," said Weeny.

They had just settled down for a teeny tiny snooze when the ground started shaking. What on Earth was happening?

Itsy and Weeny
opened their eyes
and looked up …

and up …

and up.

Itsy looked down at
the picture of the pet on the screen.
Oops!
"I think we've found our pet,"
said Itsy.
"But it's the size of our planet!"
squeaked Weeny.

Chapter Four

Itsy looked up at the giant pet.

"Perhaps," said Itsy, "we'd better *ask* it if it would like to go to Zap."

"You're right," said Weeny. "It's only polite, after all."

So Itsy got out the Teeny Tiny Translator and Megaphone.

"We are Itsy and Weeny Teeny Tiny from the planet Zap. Would you like to travel home with us in our spaceship?"

"Pleased to meet you, Itsy and Weeny. My name is Eric. I've always wanted to meet some Teeny Tiny Aliens and visit another planet," he said.

What luck!

So Itsy and Weeny got out their Teeny Tiny Collapsible Measuring Device and, with the help of the ziplets, they measured Eric. Then they measured their Teeny Tiny Spaceship.

Oops!
Eric would never fit inside.

"Perhaps we can tie him on top of our spaceship?" said Weeny.

"Or tie him underneath?" said Itsy.

"We'll just have to use the Teeny Tiny Shrink-n-Grow Machine on Eric," said Weeny, "and hope nothing goes wrong *this* time."

You see, the last time they used the
Shrink-n-Grow, they shrunk the Chief's
house by mistake.

What luck the Chief hadn't been in it!
The Chief had banned them from
using the Shrink-n-Grow Machine
ever again.

But Eric was willing to give it a go.
He really, *really* wanted to travel to
another planet.

So Itsy and Weeny used the Shrink-n-Grow Machine on Eric. Luckily, he came out just the right size to fit inside the Teeny Tiny Spaceship.

Phew! Itsy and Weeny and Eric (and the ziplets) took off for the planet Zap.

Eric was very excited to see Earth from high above. "Woo-hoo!"

When they landed on Zap, Chief
Big Teeny Tiny said, "Itsy and Weeny,
I've missed you. I forgive you for hiding
those ziplets in my birthday cake. Now
show me what you've brought back from
planet Earth."

The Chief was very excited. He'd
never seen an Eric before and he was
very keen to meet one. Luckily for Itsy
and Weeny, Eric and the Chief got on
very well.

"We're going to be best friends,"
said the Chief.

"It's like I've known you forever,"
said Eric.

"My great-great-great-great-
great-great-great-great-great-great
grandmother left Zap to look for new
planets," said the Chief. "I know she
visited Earth many Zap moons ago.
You and I might be related, Eric!" said
the Chief.

Eric was thrilled to think he might be
part Teeny Tiny Alien!

Things were going so well …

Chapter Five

The Chief invited Eric to stay at his new house.

"Make yourself at home," he said.

Eric was very impressed. He'd never seen a house before, let alone a Teeny Tiny Alien one.

"This is the teeny tiny kitchen," said the Chief. "I expect you're hungry after your trip. What do Erics eat? How about a Zap Burger and some nice blue leaves?"

Eric wasn't sure about the burger, but he tried the leaves. If he closed his eyes, they tasted just like Earth ones. Yummy. Eric finished off all the leaves and looked around for some more. The Chief had some nice-looking ones growing on his windowsill. Eric ate those as well.

"And this is the teeny tiny bubble tub and shower room," said the Chief.

Eric wasn't sure he liked the look of the bubble tub. The water looked very soapy. He took a drink. Yuk – it tasted horrid!

But the 'warm rain coming down
out of the sky' thing looked fun. Eric
stepped in. Soon he was squirting water
everywhere and singing very loudly.

It was nearly bedtime before the Chief
could get Eric out of the shower.

"And this is where you can sleep,"
said the Chief. "Itsy and Weeny and the
ziplets will keep you company. You can
have a teeny tiny sleepover. That will be
fun, won't it?"

Eric had never seen a teeny tiny bed
before. On Earth, he slept on a fresh pile
of leaves ... then ate them for breakfast
the next morning.

He jumped on the bed. It was very springy. Boing! Boing! Boing! Itsy and Weeny jumped on too. So did the ziplets. Even the Chief had a go.

Things were going brilliantly!

The next day, the Chief took Eric and Itsy and Weeny (and the ziplets) out in the Big Zapmobile. And everywhere they went, Teeny Tinies came out to cheer and wave. They'd never seen an Eric before.

That evening Eric, Chief Big Teeny Tiny and Itsy and Weeny (and the ziplets) were on the Teeny Tiny TV news.

"Phew," thought Itsy and Weeny. The Chief wouldn't banish them *ever* again, would he? Not now they were Teeny Tiny TV stars.

Chapter Six

Itsy and Weeny were feeling cheerful. Days and *days* had gone by and the Chief hadn't lost his temper once! In fact, he seemed to be in a very good mood. Even when Eric ate all the plants in the Chief's teeny tiny garden, he'd just smiled and said, "What luck! Now I don't need to do any gardening."

And when Eric drank all the water
from the Chief's garden pond he'd said,
"What luck! The pool needed cleaning
out anyway."

But the Chief did get a *teeny tiny* bit
cross when Eric got stuck in the front
seat of the Zapmobile. It took the Chief,
Itsy *and* Weeny ages to pull him out.

"You're getting fat, Eric," the
Chief said.

Poor Eric. It wasn't *his* fault. He seemed to be very hungry these days. It was getting to be a tight squeeze in the shower too. And only yesterday he'd jumped on the bed and broken it! What was going on?

Itsy and Weeny had an idea of what the problem might be. They weren't going to tell anyone, though. Not yet, anyway. Not until things got *really* bad and there were big problems with Eric.

"We shrank Eric with the Shrink-n-Grow machine, but only for a little while. Soon he'll be back to his *real* size," said Weeny.

"The size of our planet," said Itsy.

"Yes. Then the Chief will be really, *really* mad. This time, we might get banished for good," said Weeny.

Chief Big Teeny Tiny stopped being
cheerful when Eric accidentally sat on
the Zapmobile and squashed it flat.
He started to look cross when Eric
tried to get through the front door
of the house … and left a great big
Eric-shaped hole in the wall.

But he looked very, *very* cross indeed
when Eric went swimming in the Teeny Tiny
Sea and whooshed so much water
out there was hardly any left!

"Right, you pesky Teeny Tinies!" said the Chief. "Tell me what's going on."

"It's not Eric's fault. We had to use the Shrink-n-Grow machine to make him fit in the Teeny Tiny Spaceship. He was quite big, you see," said Itsy.

Oops!

They hadn't told the Chief about the shrinking.

"*How* big was Eric before you shrank him?" the Chief asked.

"Quite big," said Itsy.

"Bigger than he is now," said Weeny.

The Chief gave them a fierce stare.

"About the size of our planet," said Itsy in a very squeaky voice.

The Chief didn't speak for quite a long time. He'd gone a deep purple colour, and he looked like he might explode.

"Right, well, you'll have to shrink him again. I'm very fond of Eric, so I hope nothing goes wrong this time. Then you must take him straight back to his home planet. Maybe you two could stay on Earth with Eric. How would you like that?"

Itsy and Weeny didn't want to stay on Earth. They loved Zap. They didn't want to use the Shrink-n-Grow machine on Eric, either. Supposing this time they shrank him too much?

But Eric was very brave. He gave Itsy and Weeny a hug with his trunk.

"Do it! I've had a brilliant time on Zap," he said, "but I *really* miss Earth. I want to go home and see my family."

So they zapped Eric and held their breath.

Phew! Eric shrank to a perfect teeny tiny size!

Soon Itsy and Weeny and Eric (and the ziplets) landed back on Earth. They stepped out into the forest of green.

"I've had a brilliant time being small," Eric said, looking around. "But I'd really like to be big now, before something eats me!"

Itsy and Weeny looked at the Shrink-n-Grow Machine.

"We've never actually *grown* anything before, Eric."

"Do it!" said Eric, giving them a big smile.

So Itsy and Weeny zapped Eric with the Shrink-n-Grow machine.

What luck! Now Eric was a proper-sized elephant again.

"If only we could go back home to Zap," said Itsy.

"We can't. The Chief was very cross," said Weeny.

"Crosser than he's ever been before," said Itsy.

"What if we promise *never* to do anything silly *ever* again?" said Weeny.

"And *mean* it this time," said Itsy.

Eric shook his head and sighed. He loved Itsy and Weeny. He wanted them to be happy … on Zap.

Just then, Itsy's Teeny Tiny Space Phone pinged. Itsy and Weeny held their breath. What was the Chief going to say?

"Grrrr! You two make me so angry," he said, "but you *are* family and I miss you. So you can come home ... but leave that pesky Shrink-n-Grow machine behind with Eric!"

So Itsy and Weeny gave Eric
the Shrink-n-Grow Machine.

"Look after it, won't
you?" said Weeny.

"Promise you won't
forget us!" said Itsy.

"Elephants never
forget," said Eric, "and
the Shrink-n-Grow is quite
safe with me."

Then Itsy and Weeny
(and the ziplets) waved
goodbye to Eric and
took off in their Teeny
Tiny Spaceship. Soon
they were back home
on Zap. Chief Big Teeny
Tiny was very pleased to see them and
they all had a *great* big hug.

Itsy and Weeny (and the ziplets) were happy. The Chief was smiling and happy. Itsy and Weeny had promised not to be silly ever again … and the Shrink-n-Grow Machine was far, far away!

"I expect Eric is happy too, now he's back safely on Earth," said Itsy.

"I bet he's having a nice quiet little nap right this minute," said Weeny.

"After all his exciting adventures," said the Chief.

Oops!

After reading activities

Quick quiz

See how fast you can answer these questions!
Look back at the story if you can't remember.

⭐ **1** Which planet are the Teeny Tiny Aliens from?

⭐ **2** What illness does the Chief have at the start of the story?

⭐ **3** How do the Teeny Tiny Aliens make Eric the right size to fit in their spaceship?

Talk about it!

- Do you think the Shrink-n-Grow Machine will be safe on Earth with Eric? Why, or why not?

- If you had a Shrink-n-Grow Machine, what would you use it on?

63

1) Zap; 2) spiffle spots; 3) they use the Teeny Tiny Shrink-n-Grow Machine